Brave Little Chick

Beverley Gooding

ORCHARD BOOKS

To Nick, Jack and Rhiannon, with love – B.G.

ORCHARD BOOKS
96 Leonard Street, London EC2A 4XD
Orchard Books Australia
32/45-51 Huntley Street, Alexandria, NSW 2015
ISBN 1 84362 029 4 (hardback)
ISBN 1 84362 288 2 (paperback)
First published in Great Britain in 2003
First paperback publication in 2004
Text and illustrations © Beverley Gooding 2003
The right of Beverley Gooding to be identified as the author and
illustrator of this work has been asserted by her in accordance
with the Copyright, Designs and Patents Act, 1988.
A CIP catalogue record for this book is available
from the British Library.
(hardback) 10 9 8 7 6 5 4 3 2 1
(paperback) 10 9 8 7 6 5 4 3 2 1
Printed in Belgium

One day, a van was on its way to Bleakdale Farm.
Inside was a crate full of tiny chicks.

Suddenly, the back door flew open...

...and the crate fell out.

Quickly, the driver put the chicks back in the van, and drove on. But one very fluffy chick had bounced on to the road and tumbled into a ditch...

Fluffy Chick was all alone!
She cheeped and cheeped but
her friends didn't come back.

Then two noses appeared over the ditch.
"Hello," said Dog. "What are you doing down there?"
"I've been left behind," replied Fluffy Chick.
"Would you like to be rescued?" asked Pig.
"Yes, please!" said Fluffy Chick.

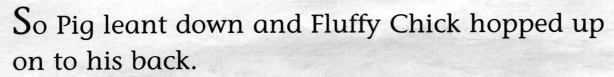

So Pig leant down and Fluffy Chick hopped up
on to his back.

"Where were you going?" asked Dog.

"Bleakdale Farm," replied Fluffy Chick.

"Oh!" snorted Pig. "You've had a lucky escape.
Farmer Bleakdale doesn't care if his hens are
cold or hungry."

"You can stay on
our farm," said Pig.
"Farmer Merryacre loves animals."
"He's very kind," agreed Dog.
Fluffy Chick liked the sound of Farmer
Merryacre, so she decided to stay.

Very soon Pig, Dog and Fluffy Chick became
the best of friends.

Fluffy Chick helped Dog to dig holes.

Dog told stories to Fluffy Chick while Pig was in the mud bath.

They had great adventures and lucky escapes.

And they always shared.

But every night, Fluffy Chick thought
about her friends at Bleakdale Farm.
She knew she had to do something.
   "Wake up!" she cheeped. "I need a plan."

"What kind of plan?" asked Dog.

"A very daring rescue plan," replied Fluffy Chick.

"I like that sort of plan," said Pig. "Leave it to me."

And Pig began to think of a plan.

At last Pig said, "I have an idea. We'll need lots of mud,
and there will be lots of digging!"

"Good," said Dog, "I like digging."
"We'll leave tonight," said Pig.

When the moon was full, Pig's plan was put into action. The three friends set out across fields, along hedgerows and over muddy ditches until they reached Bleakdale Farm.

"We'll have to burrow under the fence," said Pig. So they all began to dig.

At the henhouse, the chicks cheeped with delight to see their friend.

"Shush," said Dog, "you'll wake Farmer Bleakdale."

"We've come to rescue you," whispered Fluffy Chick. "You'll never be cold or hungry again."

"Follow me," said Pig.

So the hens and chicks followed
Pig, Dog and Fluffy Chick across fields,
along hedgerows and through ditches so muddy,
that by the time they reached Merryacre Farm...

...there was not a white hen to be seen.

"We can sleep here," whispered Pig, as he led the tired chicks and muddy hens into the warm barn. "You'll be safe with us," said Dog.

"And cosy," yawned Fluffy Chick.

Next morning, Dog woke with a start. He could hear a loud voice outside and stomping footsteps.

"It's Farmer Bleakdale!" said Pig. "He's getting closer!"

At that moment, the barn door
flew open and there stood Farmer Bleakdale!

Farmer Bleakdale was angry!
"Where are my white hens?" he snarled,
stomping into the barn.

"STOP THERE!" called a voice. It was Farmer Merryacre. "Leave the hens alone. We only have brown hens here."

"Off my farm this minute!" said Farmer Merryacre, marching Farmer Bleakdale away. "And don't ever come back!"

"Hooray!" said Pig, Dog and Fluffy Chick.
"Hooray!" said all the chicks and hens.

At last they were safe.

Fluffy Chick told all her friends to make
themselves at home on Merryacre Farm.

And so they did!